Edith L. Dalton

More Rhymes

Edith L. Dalton

More Rhymes

ISBN/EAN: 9783337265588

Printed in Europe, USA, Canada, Australia, Japan

Cover: Foto ©Andreas Hilbeck / pixelio.de

More available books at **www.hansebooks.com**

RHYMES

BY EDITH LEVERETT DALTON

"Short poems which show a considerable power of poetical conception."—*The Congregationalist*, Boston.

"Miss Dalton has the poetic instinct. Her verse is tender, thoughtful and sincere."—*Cambridge Tribune*.

"Her little songs are refreshingly free from morbid sentiment and cloudy mysticism."—*The Bowdoin Orient*, Brunswick.

"She is most fortunate in her choice of themes."—*Portland Transcript*.

"The verses show absolute sincerity and directness and true poetic feeling."—*The Citizen*, Philadelphia.

"There is a certain tender charm over everything."—*The Protestant Episcopal Review*, Richmond.

MORE RHYMES

BY EDITH LEVERETT

DALTON

BOSTON

DAMRELL & UPHAM

The Old Corner Bookstore

283, Washington Street

1899

PRESS OF
HUNTLEY S. TURNER
AYER

MORE RHYMES

TO MY MOTHER.

When life tenderly was dawning,
My eyes opened on thy face,
And my heart awoke that morning
In the warmth of thine embrace.
All the world around unheeding,
I yet felt thy love and smiled—
Ah! Throughout the years succeeding,
Thou hast never failed thy child.

THE CRADLE.

Well have we loved this little earth,
  The cradle of our kind,
But shall we sorrow that erelong
  It will be left behind ?

"THEN SHALL I KNOW."

I read these pages when I was a child,
Eagerly on the book my heart was bent,
But though my tears were stirred and though
      I smiled,
The baby mind could not know what was
      meant.

Here is the book, my love, my little child,
Read, and the understanding shall be sent—
O Life !   Not vainly have we sighed or smiled,
We shall yet understand what it has meant.

TO FRIEND WHITTIER.

In the sweet stir of April days
  I often think of thee—
The earth is wakening to praise,
And well I know that all thy ways
  Are full of melody.

Dear Poet ! Thou hast read aright
  The meaning of the Spring,
For what were dim to other sight
Thou seest by the inner light
  That gladdens everything.

FANCY FREE.

Never saw I many,
Never loved I any,
  My heart is my own.
While the sun shines brightly,
I am tripping lightly
  Into the unknown.

DESIRE.

O that I could find favour in thy sight!
For thou art as the breath of life to me,
Thou swayest my being as the wind the sea—
If thou wert mine, then would my arm have
      might
To steer through all the storms that threaten
      thee.

FLUTTERINGS.

Alas! I know not if I read aright
The look which thou art bending upon me—
How can I know if this new thrill be blight,
Or bloom? Day after day, night after night,
I hush my heart, lulling the thought of thee.

TO A BRIDE.

(WITH THE GIFT OF A BOOT-HOOK.)

Need I wish a pleasant pathway
For the pressing of thy feet?
Since the way will not be lonely,
Sure the journey shall be sweet.

THE SAILOR AND THE MAIDEN.

THE SAILOR.

I once was a rover,
    My fancies were bright,
I sailed the seas over
    In search of delight.

THE MAIDEN.

I looked from my window
    Across the broad sea,
I saw thy sail coming—
    It came unto me.

THE SAILOR.

Now my voyages are over,
  My fancies are past,
And the heart of the rover
  To thee is made fast.

THE MAIDEN.

I care not to be famous,
  Or wealthy, or clever,
My life has one purpose,
  I love thee forever.

LAY OF A LOST HEART.

"I'd a heart I meant to keep,
   It has gone astray, Sir."
"Little Bo-Peep, who lost her sheep,
   Will show you your best way, Sir."

" Little Bo-Peep, where must I roam
   To find the heart that's straying?"
"'Let it alone, it'll come home,'
   That's what folk were saying."

" Blessings on your friendly crook,
   And may your sheep be thronging!
In truth you look wise as a book—
   Little Bo-Peep, Good-morning."

GOLDENROD.

"O Goldenrod, what do you here
  While it is but July?
Remind me not that Fall is near,
  Wait until by and by.

" O Goldenrod, I pr'ythee wait—"
  She tosses a reply,
"Ah, you may tarry till too late,
  But never so will I ! "

INDIAN SUMMER.

Our fathers felt hoar-frost and drew
 Around the fire, saying
"Now snow will fall to cover all
 Until we go a-maying."

'Twas then the Indian shook his head—
 "No, no," said he, "More summer."
"Oh, can it be," they asked, "that we
 May look for such a comer?"

And, while they wondered, they beheld
 The summertide returning,
More sweetly near, more deeply dear
 Than when hot suns were burning.

So when we think of joy as gone,
    And grief as the next comer,
Let us believe we need not grieve—
    There cometh Indian Summer !

LAUREL.

O thou from whom our love cannot be parted,
Around my thought of thee I wind a wreath,
For thou hast gone through life as one great-
       hearted,
Seeking the deeper meaning underneath.

For thou hast won that which is worth the
       winning,
Without whose touch in vain our seasons roll,
That peace of which we have but the begin-
       ning,
And which is aye the summer of the soul.

THE PLANT ON THE WINDOW–SEAT.

Chill is the little pane of glass
Through which the storm is seen,
Yet to that wintry light they turn,
Those leaves of gladsome green.

The storm is sailing out to sea,
Again the sun shines forth,
And now a flower blooms beside
My window in the North.

RHYME

READ AT A MEETING OF THE BEE.

Oft have I looked around from friend to friend,
Wishing for skill by which might be portrayed
The charms that have so fair a gathering
      made,
And ever, while my homeward way I wend,
I see the girls as with them I had stayed.

Before me rises, beautiful in height,
With locks radiant as the golden fleece,
And blue eyes beaming blessing without cease,
Louise, whose presence sheds a starry light,
And in whose sweet serenity is peace.

I see a noble face whose every line
Reveals the ardour of the soul within,
For Sally's nature knows not wavering,
And her enthusiasm most divine
Shall many a heart to truth and heaven win.

What fun is lurking in those merry eyes
That yet can look so tender if need be !
We all trust Grace—no summer friend is she,
More surely than suns set or moons arise,
She cares for us in her sincerity.

As a light-hearted song cheerily sung
Refreshes him who listens to the lay,
And helps him bear the burden of the day,
So joyously does our Beth move among
Her neighbours, making melody alway.

Then there is Patience with her winsome face,
And tresses fit to charm a painter's eye—
How like a fairy she goes flitting by,
Her every movement full of dainty grace,
And witchery alike in smile or sigh !

Ah, Julia !   Not a girl repeats her name
Without feeling a thrill of friendliness
For her whose yes means no, and no means
   yes,
The perverse one, whom none of us can tame,
But who is dear to all, nevertheless.

And here is one who ever thoughtful seems,
The depths of her dark eyes have power to
   please,
Who looks into her face much meaning sees—
While the far strains that are heard in her
   dreams,
We hear when Helen's fingers touch the keys.

How often have our eyes sought Anna's cheek,
Delighting in its beauty! And we feel
That in her bosom beats a heart as leal
As one could find who through the world
      should seek,
A generous heart to which we can appeal.

Who speaks not well of Alice! Excellence
Like hers, however, who can duly praise!
It shines in all her words, in all her ways—
" Strength and honour are her clothing,"
      Hence
We read " She shall rejoice in future days."

Bright is the bloom of our Elizabeth,
And she has aspirations which inspire
The life whose earnestness we all admire,
And the deft hand that, guided by their breath,
Ever seeks to express her heart's desire.

Though Mary may be many miles away,
Her presence lingers at our meetings yet.
She is a girl whom no one could forget—
We shall not meet her like in many a day,
For one so rare as she is seldom met.

Carrie still comes to us, a welcome guest,
And from her home, as wife and mother
    should,
She brings an influence so true, so good,
That we rejoice she is thus deeply blessed
In the fulfilment of her womanhood.

Again we meet as in the happy past,
Again the dear, familiar group we see—
O days that are to come! Through woe and
    glee
We stand together, faithful to the last,
Our love forever loyal to the Bee.

TO A KNOCKER.

Yes, as thou ever mindest me,
  When peace was won by war,
The brave old General built this house
  And put thee on the door.

Thou hast announced the patriot,
  The captain home from sea,
The lover, whose heart beat aloud
  Though scarce he lifted thee.

Thou hast seen Henry Wadsworth go
  To storm Tripoli's walls,
And hast beheld his namesake leave
  For Bowdoin's quiet halls.

The friends who mourned young Wadsworth's
    death
  Came knocking, long ago,
And they that welcomed back again
  The gentle Longfellow.

I need not take thee in my hand—
  So eloquent thou art,
That if I only look on thee
  Thou knockest in my heart.

FAITHFUL STEWARDS.

They have done and are departing,
On whom we have leaned so long,
In the strength of whose endeavour
Has the city, too, been strong.

He who, standing in the pulpit,
Fed the people with the Word,
While from house to house his message
From the Prince of Peace was heard,—

He who taught the trooping children,
Trained them how to live by rule,
Filling them with inspiration
For the life beyond the school,—

He who in the daily paper
Calmed the passions of the crowd,
Till the whisper of his conscience
Through the land was heard aloud,—.

He who in the court of justice,
Still the stronghold of the weak,
With no fear of man before him,
In the fear of God did speak,—

He who ever came to succour,
From the day that we drew breath,
Who in the night-watches wrestled
For us, hand to hand with death,—

He to whom the toiling thousands
Turned, and did not turn in vain,
As he bore the weight of commerce
Through the panic's stress and strain,—

He who when our hearts were failing,
When we only heard a moan,
Led the burst of heavenly music,
Like to that before the throne,—

They have done and are departing,
On whom we have leaned so long,
In the strength of whose endeavour
Has the city, too, been strong.

Send us men to make the future,
Men to lead the onward way!
Rise up early, Lord, and send them,
For there dawns another day.

A VIGIL.

1898.

O God, Who knowest that we went
Unflinchingly into the fight
Because most earnestly we meant
What is accepted in Thy sight,

Strengthen the arms that strike for law,
And let the flag which is unfurled
Float till the nations know we war
For the well-being of the world,—

Hasten the day when strife shall cease,
When all shall be as brethren blest,
And in each bosom may the peace
Which passeth understanding rest.

ON A PICTURE

OF A BOY AFTERWARD AN OFFICER

IN THE ARMY OF THE POTOMAC.

O thou dear child looking out upon life, un-
 afraid,
What are the years that are hid
    from those wondering eyes?
For what in the fathomless counsels of God
 wert thou made
 Thus joyously strong, heavenly wise?

We are one people still in these waxing days,
Lord, make us worthy of this
    for which he died—
So, like the Master to Whom his death gave
 praise,
 He shall see of his travail, satisfied.

THE CONFEDERATES OF VIRGINIA.

"Who can forget them?"

Address at Reunion
of the Army of the Potomac.

Never were nobler hearts—
      Ah, not in vain
They met the northern host,
      Whose love was won.
Saddest of wars!
      Our tears have quenched in rain
Thine embers.
      On thy glory shines the sun.

DOROTHY STURDIVANT.

Beneath the boughs of an elm-shaded street,
Her blue eyes first looked out on our earth,
Through their long lashes, and she found life
    sweet,
For she could feel its sweetness from her birth.
Beyond earth opened Heaven, for when she
    heard
Her father preach her heart received the word.

He went to feed a flock beside the sea,
Where the white ships were sailing to the
    strand,
Borne upon tranquil tides that tenderly
Came up and kissed the slopes of meadowland.
And here to womanhood Dorothy grew,
Here love, marriage and motherhood she
    knew.

Then the long lashes fell upon her cheeks,
And the blue eyes shed their young light no
      more—
But still the halo round her name bespeaks
What once she was in the dear days of yore.
While by her grave we look out on the sea,
And thought is rapt into Eternity.

MARGARET.

She had the lips of which we dream,
The rare, the perfect lips that seem
        Fit portals
For tender smile and speech and song
Which stir in us the hopes of strong
        Immortals.

It came, the looked-for, longed-for smile,
And dwelt upon her lips awhile,
        Expressing
Such love as makes the angels sing,
True love, that ever comes to bring
        A blessing.

Day after day and all day long,
She tuned her voice for speech and song
                    By trilling
Those little notes which, though apart
From our language, through the heart
                    Go thrilling.

But ere she spoke her soul had flown,
And now she sings before the throne—
                    Ah, never
Will we forget, though waiting long,
We shall have smile and speech and song
                    Forever !

A RHYME FOR CHRISTMASTIDE.

It was when chill December blew
  His blasts throughout the land,
When blossoming shrubs no longer grew,
  And Christmas was at hand.

There was a maid called Margery
  Who sat beside the fire,
And wrought in colours on her knee
  Till heart and hands did tire.

She dropped her hands into her lap,
  Her heart she could not rest
Until she fell into a nap,
  Which quieted her breast.

She dreamed that it was Christmas Day,
 And all her gifts were done—
Upon the window-seat they lay,
 She touched them, one by one.

The room was dressed with evergreen,
 While that which glistened so
Was what each other Yule had seen,
 The branch of mistletoe.

How dark and gloomy looked the fir !
 How cold the wintertide !
The mistletoe recalled to her
 Something at which she sighed.

She drew her hood around her face,
 Her cloak about her form,
She started at a hurried pace,
 Whirled onward by the storm.

The sky was white, the ground was white,
  The air was full of snow,
She could not hear her footfall light
  That trampled it below.

Something within her seemed to say,
  She knew not how nor why,
" Thou hast a need, a need to-day "—
  And her heart answered "Ay."

As she drew near the church, there came
  The voices of the throng,
Dwelling upon the Saviour's name
  In an outburst of song.

It was a hymn she knew of old,
  And all her nature stirred
While like the fullest tide it rolled,
  Comfort in every word.

" Shout the glad tidings, exultingly sing,
Jerusalem triumphs, Messiah is King!"

Her heart and the organ together were swell-
    ing—
"The Son of the Highest, how lowly His
    birth!"
The story that Christians forever are telling,
" He stoops to redeem thee, He reigns upon
    earth.

" Shout the glad tidings, exultingly sing,
Jerusalem triumphs, Messiah is King!"

O marvellous message!   " From nation to
    nation,
The heart-cheering news let the earth echo
    round,
How free to the faithful He offers salvation "—
Ah, why then need sorrow, not gladness,
    abound!

"Shout the glad tidings, exultingly sing,
Jerusalem triumphs, Messiah is King!

"Mortals, your homage be gratefully bring-
ing,"
Yes, let the whole heart for His service arise,
Our lives He shall ever to glory be winging,
"One chorus resound through the earth and
the skies!

"Shout the glad tidings, exultingly sing,
Jerusalem triumphs, Messiah is King!"

When Margery awoke, the day
Had disappeared and all was gray.
The fire was low, to outer sight
Things sadder looked than in the light.

But Margery arose and drew
With cheerful hand the curtain to—
Pleasant embroidery seemed to her,
Pleasant the mistletoe and fir.

She rung no bell, but lit herself
The lamp, stepped softly to the shelf,
And got the book upon whose page
Hope speaks aloud to every age.

She read of Him Who, born to reign,
Hath triumphed over sin and pain,
A Lord, a Saviour and a Friend,
Of Whose great rule shall be no end.

SAINT STEPHEN'S.

The sunlight falls across thine aisles
Through windows coloured by the past,
By precious memories that last
Like comfort given us by smiles.
And we who have gone through the years
Together, heart revealing heart
To one another, kneel,—apart
From all our earthly cares and fears.

We feel the thrill of common prayer,
And thy gray walls no longer stand
Around us, but on every hand
The worship of the world we share.
Nor does thy roof shut out the sky,
But, looking upward, we behold
The Heaven Stephen saw unfold
Her pearly gates as he drew nigh.

And when the vision is fulfilled,
When we are with that throng which none
Can number, where they need no sun,
Nor need they any temple build,—
When with the host of Heaven we pour
Our worship, we shall think of thee,
Remembering through eternity
Where first our hearts learned to adore.